Victoria Roberts Deborah Allwright

Peculiar
Pets

ALISON GREEN BOOKS

Mum, can I have a pet?
Please?
Mum, Mum, can I?
Can I have a pet?

We'll see.

So I see . . .
I see a rock. A smooth rock.
I put string around it.

I call him **Fluffy.**

I take **Fluffy** for walks.

I let him off his lead
if he's good.

And he's good . . . for a day or two.

Mum, can I have a pet? **Please?**
Mum, Mum, can I?
Can I have a pet?

We'll see.

So I see . . .
I see a glove.
A soft woolly glove.

I put it in a basket.
I call her **Nibbles**.

I tickle Nibbles
in her basket.

I feed her
whenever she's hungry.

And she's hungry . . .

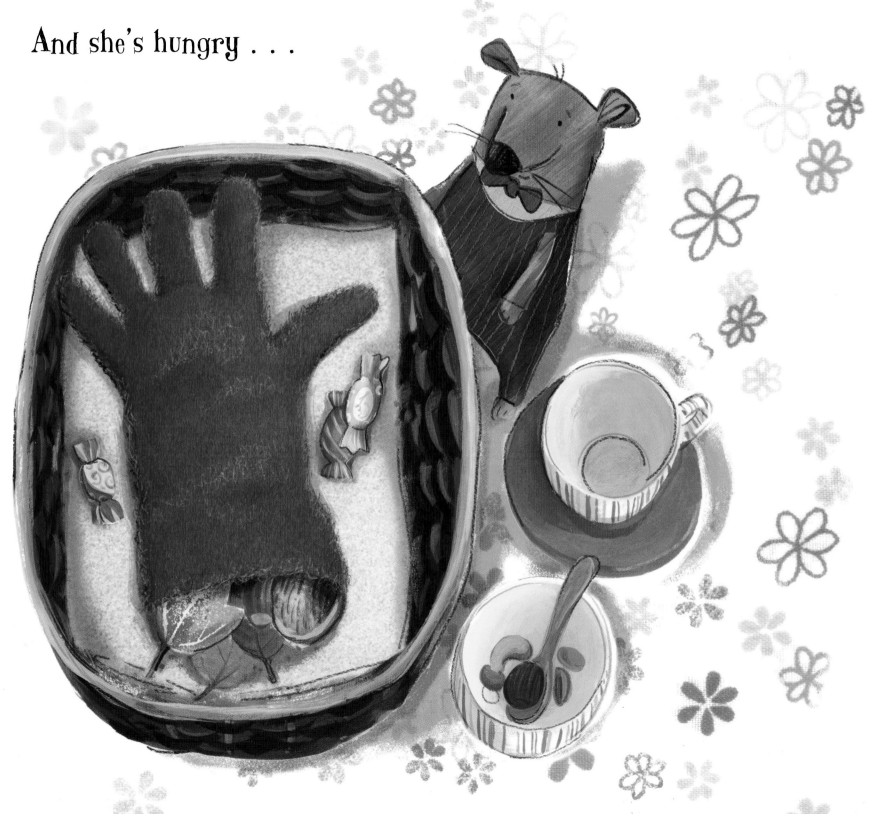

for a day or two.

Mum, can I have a pet?
Please?
Mum, Mum, can I?
Can I have a pet?

We'll see.

So I see . . .

I see a sweet wrapper.
A shiny sweet wrapper.

I put it in a bowl.
I call him **William**.

I give William water.
I see him twist and turn as he swims.

And he swims . . .

for a day or two.

Mum, can I have a pet? **Please?**
Mum, Mum, can I?
Can I have a pet?

We'll see.

So I see . . .
I see a balloon.
A round balloon.

I draw a face on it.
I call him BRUCE.

I stroke Bruce.

And he sticks to me
when we hug.

And we hug . . .

And we play . . .

And we dance about . . .
And Bruce is my best pet ever . . .

for a day or two.

Oh, that's a pity.
Never mind.
Perhaps we can find another
pet for you to play with.

Let's see . . .

So we see . . .

We see a box.
A cardboard box.
We lift the lid.
We peep inside.

And we see . . .

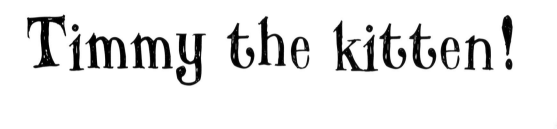

Timmy the kitten!

And Timmy is the best pet

in the world!